INFOMOJIS

PLANET EARTH

WAYLAND
www.waylandbooks.co.uk

First published in Great Britain
in 2018 by Wayland
Copyright © Hodder and Stoughton, 2018
All rights reserved

Editor: Amy Pimperton
Produced by Tall Tree Ltd
Editor: Jon Richards
Designer: Ed Simkins

ISBN: 978 1 5263 0701 9

Wayland
An imprint of Hachette Children's Group
Part of Hodder and Stoughton
Carmelite House
50 Victoria Embankment
London EC4Y 0DZ

An Hachette UK Company
www.hachette.co.uk
www.hachettechildrens.co.uk

Printed and bound in China

MIX
Paper from
responsible sources
FSC® C104740
FSC
www.fsc.org

This book uses different units to measure different things:

Distance is measured in kilometres (km), metres (m), centimetres (cm) and
millimetres (mm).

Volume is measured using cubic kilometres (cubic km).

Temperature is measured in degrees Celsius (°C).

Mass is measured in tonnes and gigatonnes (a gigatonne is 1 billion tonnes).

Power is measure in petawatts (a petawatt is 1 quadrillion watts).

FORMATION OF EARTH 4

EARTH'S PLACE IN SPACE..................... 6

WHAT'S INSIDE EARTH? 8

EARTH'S CHANGING FACE 10

A VIOLENT PLANET........................ 12

BUILDING MOUNTAINS

AND VALLEYS...............................14

MAKING ROCKS............................ 16

SHAPING ROCKS 18

THE ATMOSPHERE........................ 20

WINDS AND WEATHER.....................22

THE WATER CYCLE........................ 24

HABITATS..................................26

CLIMATE CHANGE 28

GLOSSARY 30

INDEX 32

FORMATION OF EARTH

About 4.6 billion years ago, Earth was a collection of small pieces of dust and rock that formed a large disc of material orbiting the young Sun. These pieces of dust and rock collected together, forming the new planet.

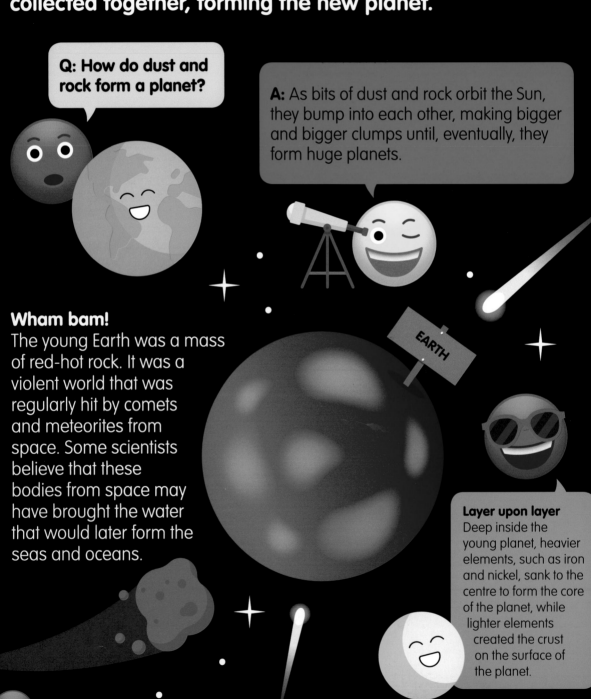

Q: How do dust and rock form a planet?

A: As bits of dust and rock orbit the Sun, they bump into each other, making bigger and bigger clumps until, eventually, they form huge planets.

EARTH

Wham bam!
The young Earth was a mass of red-hot rock. It was a violent world that was regularly hit by comets and meteorites from space. Some scientists believe that these bodies from space may have brought the water that would later form the seas and oceans.

Layer upon layer
Deep inside the young planet, heavier elements, such as iron and nickel, sank to the centre to form the core of the planet, while lighter elements created the crust on the surface of the planet.

Forming the Moon

Billions of years ago, the young Earth was hit by a very large object. Astronomers believe that this object was about the size of Mars. It slammed into Earth, throwing up a huge amount of rocky material. This material clumped together to form the Moon.

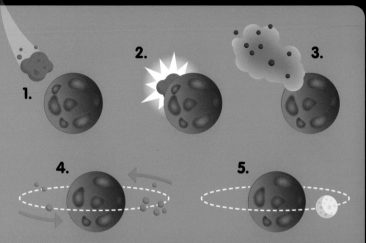

1.
2.
3.
4.
5.

Cooling planet

Over time, Earth cooled and a layer of gases formed around the planet, protecting it from many further impacts. The earliest continents formed and conditions became ideal for life to start.

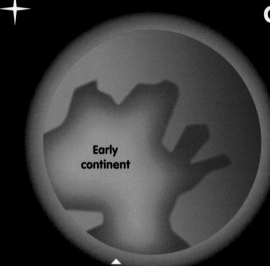

Early continent

Layer of gases

Life appears

The first living things were tiny, single-celled organisms that may have appeared more than 4.2 billion years ago. They may have been simple, but they dominated life on Earth for the next 2 billion years.

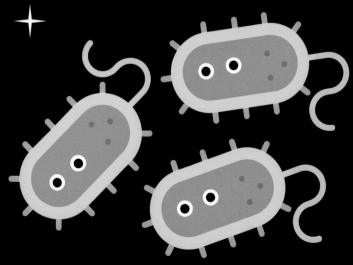

EARTH'S PLACE IN SPACE

Earth is the third planet from the Sun, about 150 million kilometres from the shining star. At this distance, it's in just the right place for something wonderful to happen – it's the only place we know of in the Universe where life has evolved and thrives!

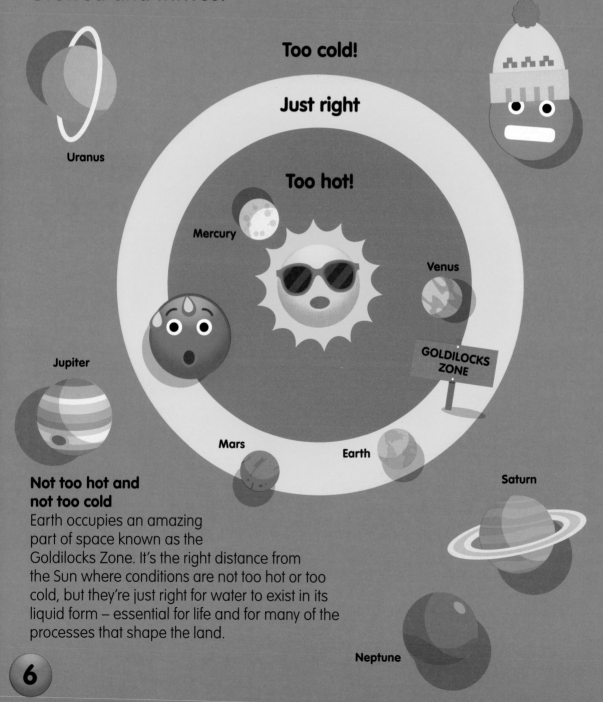

Too cold!

Just right

Too hot!

Uranus

Mercury

Venus

Jupiter

GOLDILOCKS ZONE

Mars

Earth

Saturn

Neptune

Not too hot and not too cold

Earth occupies an amazing part of space known as the Goldilocks Zone. It's the right distance from the Sun where conditions are not too hot or too cold, but they're just right for water to exist in its liquid form – essential for life and for many of the processes that shape the land.

Other Goldilocks zones
Astronomers estimate that there may be as many as 40 billion planets that orbit in the Goldilocks Zones of other stars in our Milky Way galaxy.

Solar power

174 petawatts –
The amount of power reaching Earth's upper atmosphere from the Sun. (A petawatt is equivalent to one quadrillion watts.)

Thirty per cent of this is reflected back into space. Seventy per cent is absorbed by clouds, oceans and the land.

Lights in the sky
The Sun throws out a stream of charged particles. Earth's magnetic field channels these particles to the polar regions where they interact with particles in the air, creating the beautiful glowing aurorae.

Earth receives more energy from the Sun in an hour than humans use in a whole year.

The Sun's energy heats the oceans and land, which warms the air above it, causing it to churn about, driving our planet's weather (see pages 22–23).

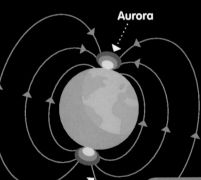

Aurora

Magnetic field

Space protector
Other objects in the Solar System may play a part in protecting Earth, making it ideal for life. Some astronomers believe that Jupiter's powerful gravity stops some comets from getting too close to Earth, either flinging them back out into space or causing them to crash into the giant gas planet.

WHAT'S INSIDE EARTH?

Rock solid – that's what you might think about Earth, but far beneath your feet, powerful forces churn things about.

The crust
Surrounding everything is the thin, solid crust, which contains the land and seabed. It is between 8–40 km thick.

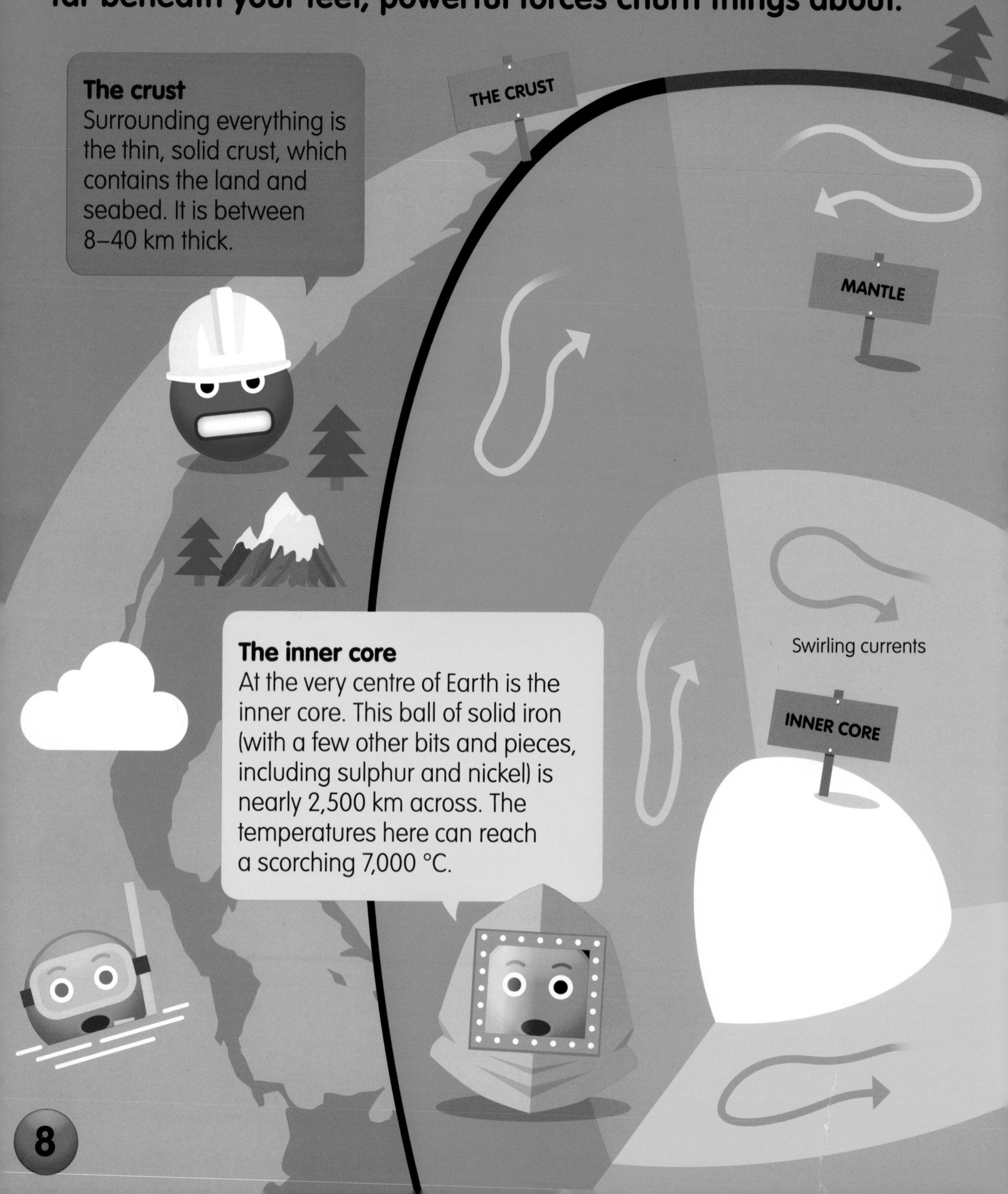

THE CRUST

MANTLE

The inner core
At the very centre of Earth is the inner core. This ball of solid iron (with a few other bits and pieces, including sulphur and nickel) is nearly 2,500 km across. The temperatures here can reach a scorching 7,000 °C.

Swirling currents

INNER CORE

The mantle

Surrounding the outer core and below the crust is a layer of rock called the mantle, which is about 2,900 km thick. Even though the mantle is superhot, it is still solid, but the temperatures are so high that the rock moves like thick road tar in enormous churning currents. Temperatures in the mantle range from 500–4,000 °C.

Q: How do we know about the structure of Earth?

A: Scientists study how seismic shockwaves from earthquakes are affected as they travel through the different thicknesses and temperatures of the various layers.

Shockwaves

The outer core

Surrounding the inner core is an outer core of liquid iron, which is about 2,300 km thick. Temperatures are a little cooler than the inner core, but they can still reach 5,000 °C.

OUTER CORE

One giant magnet

Swirling currents in the outer core create a magnetic field that turns Earth into one giant magnet. Compasses line up with this magnetic field, showing which direction north is in and helping us to find our way.

EARTH'S CHANGING FACE

Nothing stays the same – even Earth. Over millions of years, mountains are built up, valleys are gouged out and whole new continents are formed and break apart.

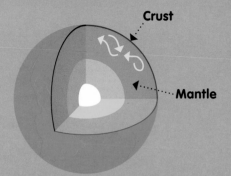

Crust

Mantle

Driving the change
The swirling currents in Earth's mantle pull and push on Earth's crust, splitting it into huge pieces called tectonic plates. These plates are pushed about and pulled apart, crashing into each other and carrying the landmasses with them.

Drifting continents
Although others had put forward the idea of moving continents hundreds of years ago, the idea of continental drift was first fully explained in 1912 by me, German scientist Alfred Wegener (1880–1930). I suggested that all of Earth's landmasses had once been joined together in one supercontinent called Pangea.

ALFRED WEGENER

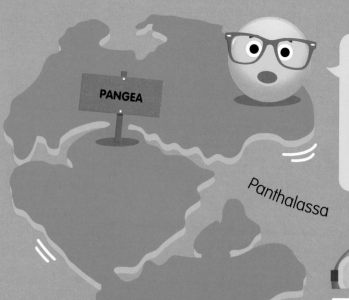

PANGEA

Panthalassa

1 – About 335 million years ago, Earth's landmasses were joined together to form a supercontinent called Pangea. It was surrounded by one huge ocean called Panthalassa.

Care for a dip?

LAURASIA

GONDWANALAND

2 – About 200 million years ago, Pangea split into two main continents, Laurasia to the north and Gondwanaland to the south.

3 – Over the next 150 million years, the continents continued to move. The Atlantic Ocean opened up between North America and Europe. South America and North America moved towards each other. India moved northwards and slammed into Asia, and Australia broke away from Antarctica.

NORTH AMERICA

EUROPE

ASIA

Atlantic Ocean

AFRICA

INDIA

SOUTH AMERICA

AUSTRALIA

ANTARCTICA

NORTH AMERICA

EURASIA (EUROPE AND ASIA)

AFRICA

SOUTH AMERICA

AUSTRALIA

ANTARCTICA

4 – Today, there are six main landmasses: North America, South America, Eurasia, Africa, Australia and Antarctica, as well as thousands of smaller islands.

11

A VIOLENT PLANET

The powerful forces that push about Earth's tectonic plates can have violent effects, shaking the ground and pushing superhot liquid rock to the surface in violent volcanic eruptions.

PLATE BOUNDARIES

Divergent – where two plates move apart, liquid rock wells up from underground to form new crust.

Convergent – where two plates crash into each other, one may be pushed down into Earth where it melts. This molten rock rises up through the crust to form volcanoes.

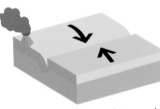

Transform – where two plates rub against each other, friction can build up, causing the plates to jar and then slip past each other with a sudden movement. This sudden release of energy creates earthquakes.

Q: Where can you find the most volcanoes?

A: Most volcanoes form at the boundaries between tectonic plates. The area with the most volcanoes on the planet is found around the Pacific Ocean where several tectonic plates meet. This area is known as the 'Ring of Fire'.

Earth shakers
The most powerful earthquake ever recorded occurred off the coast of Chile in 1960. It had a magnitude (strength) of 9.4–9.6 on the Richter Scale.

Supervolcanoes

These are enormous volcanoes. While a normal, large volcano throws out about 1 cubic km of material, a supervolcano erupts at least 1,000 cubic km of rocks and lava.

Normal volcano

A supervolcano forms a large hole, called a caldera, instead of a normal volcano cone.

Cone

Caldera

A supervolcano does not erupt that often, with hundreds of thousands of years between each eruption.

Supervolcano

Cough, cough!

USA

Yellowstone

Beneath Yellowstone in the Northwestern United States is one of the biggest supervolcanoes on the planet. It has erupted just three times in the last 3 million years, and the last eruption occurred about 630,000 years ago. The caldera of this supervolcano measures 55 by 80 km. If it erupts again, it could have catastrophic effects on the whole planet, throwing out huge clouds of dust and cooling Earth by several degrees.

BUILDING MOUNTAINS AND VALLEYS

Whether its towering peaks or deep canyons, planet Earth is continually changing as landmasses are pushed up, torn apart and worn away.

Mountain types

Volcanic mountains are peaks that have been thrown up by liquid rock welling up from deep beneath the ground. Volcanic mountains can be found as chains along the edges of tectonic plates, such as the Andes in South America, or as lonely peaks, such as those on Hawaii, USA.

Block mountains are formed when a large block of the crust is pushed up or drops down when two plates move apart, leaving the two sides as high mountain chains.

VOLCANIC MOUNTAIN

BLOCK MOUNTAIN

FOLD MOUNTAIN

Fold mountains are created when two plates slam into each other causing them to buckle and thrust upwards.

Mount Everest, found in the Himalayas in Nepal, is the world's highest mountain at 8,848 m above sea level. The first people to reach the top were Sir Edmund Hillary (1919–2008) and Tenzing Norgay (1914–1986).

They may be the highest, but the Himalayas are some of the newest kids on the mountain block.

225 million years ago, India was an island located just off the coast of Australia.

About 200 million years ago it started to drift north at a rate of up to 16 cm a year.

About 50-40 million years ago, the rate of movement slowed to about 6 cm a year as India collided with the Eurasian plate.

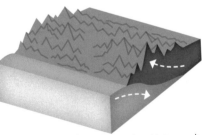

As the two landmasses pushed into each other, they crumpled and folded, pushing up to form the soaring peaks. They are still growing at a rate of about 1 cm a year.

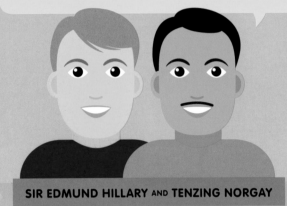

SIR EDMUND HILLARY AND TENZING NORGAY

 Well if you think that's tall, get a load of Mauna Kea. Measured from the seabed, this huge volcano in Hawaii, USA, is more that 10,000 m tall, dwarfing Mount Everest and its Himalayan friends.

Cutting valleys
As rivers and streams flow through the landscape, they cut away the rocks and soil on their banks and bed, carving out valleys and steep-sided gorges.

MAKING ROCKS

As Earth's surface changes, the rocks that make up its features are changed in a continual, but very slow process called the rock cycle.

Rock types

Igneous rocks, such as granite, form from cooling liquid rock.

Sedimentary rocks, such as sandstone, form from sediments that have settled at the bottom of a river or sea and have been squeezed together to form a hard rock.

Metamorphic rocks have been changed by intense heat or pressure.

Hot liquid rock from deep inside Earth wells up and cools or erupts onto the surface and cools to form igneous rocks.

Igneous rocks

Rocks are pushed up by tectonic movement.

Rocks are melted to form magma.

Metamorphic rocks get their name from the Greek words *meta* and *morphe*, meaning 'change of form'.

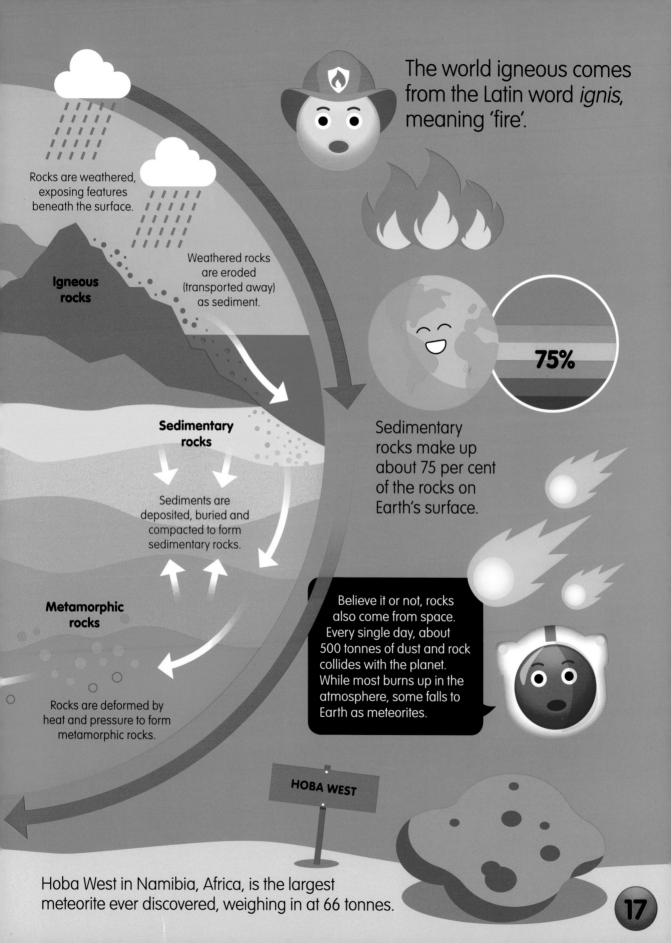

The world igneous comes from the Latin word *ignis*, meaning 'fire'.

Rocks are weathered, exposing features beneath the surface.

Igneous rocks

Weathered rocks are eroded (transported away) as sediment.

75%

Sedimentary rocks

Sediments are deposited, buried and compacted to form sedimentary rocks.

Sedimentary rocks make up about 75 per cent of the rocks on Earth's surface.

Metamorphic rocks

Believe it or not, rocks also come from space. Every single day, about 500 tonnes of dust and rock collides with the planet. While most burns up in the atmosphere, some falls to Earth as meteorites.

Rocks are deformed by heat and pressure to form metamorphic rocks.

HOBA WEST

Hoba West in Namibia, Africa, is the largest meteorite ever discovered, weighing in at 66 tonnes.

SHAPING ROCKS

Given enough time and the right conditions, even the toughest rocks can be worn away, creating amazing features that shape our landscape.

Valley

Weathering, erosion, deposition

Weathering is where rock is broken down into smaller pieces. This can be achieved mechanically (such as freezing and thawing), chemically (such as water dissolving limestone), or organically (such as when plant roots crack open rocks).

Deposition is the dropping of these eroded rock pieces by the wind or rivers in different places.

Erosion is the removal of these pieces of rock and it can be carried out by rivers, seas, ice, wind or just plain old gravity.

River features
What rivers carve out of the land depends on where they are on their path to the sea.

1. Close to its source, an active river will carve a steep-sided valley.

2. Further along, the valley will start to open out and the river will cut sideways bends, called meanders.

FLOODPLAIN

3. Near the end of its path, the river may form a wide floodplain, with broad meanders, before it empties into the sea at the river mouth.

Sediment

Glacier features

They may not be the fastest moving things on the planet, but huge glaciers can carve out some enormous features, including random boulders (erratics), U-shaped valleys and sharp-peaked horn mountains.

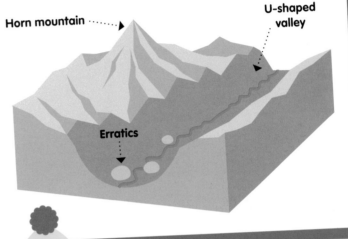

Horn mountain ·······▶

U-shaped valley

Erratics

Meander

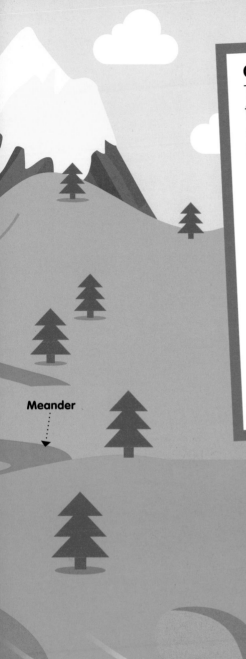

Erratic

Erratics are huge boulders that have been picked up by a glacier, carried over long distances and then dumped far from where they originated.

Rock pedestal

Wind features

The wind can pick up tiny pieces of rock. When these are hurled at stone, they can sandblast and shape it into amazing features, such as rock pedestals.

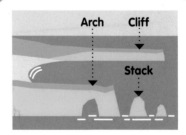

Arch   Cliff

Stack

Coastal features

With the sea constantly pounding the shore, it's no surprise that coastal rocks can form some impressive features, including cliffs, arches and stacks.

THE ATMOSPHERE

Stretching from Earth's surface and up into space is a layer of gases that protects the planet from most of the harmful radiation and rocks that come from space.

Atmosphere structure

What is the atmosphere made from?

Nitrogen 78%

Oxygen 21%

Other gases 1% (including argon, carbon dioxide, and helium)

Exosphere (700–10,000 km) is the outer layer of the atmosphere, which merges into space.

Exosphere

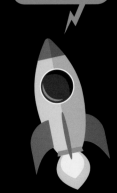

Thermosphere (80–700 km) is where the aurorae occur (see page 7) and where the Kármán Line is found – the official start of space.

The temperature in the thermosphere can reach 1,500 °C, but the gas molecules are so far apart that it would not feel hot.

Thermosphere

Mesosphere (50–80 km) is where most meteoroids burn up, creating shooting stars or meteors.

The mesosphere is the coldest place on Earth, with an average temperature of -85 °C.

Mesosphere

The top of the troposphere can vary from about 9 km above the poles to 17 km above the Equator.

Stratosphere

Stratosphere (12–50 km) contains the ozone layer, which absorbs most of the Sun's ultraviolet radiation.

Troposphere

Troposphere (0–12 km) contains about 75 per cent of the atmosphere's mass and is where most of our weather occurs.

WINDS AND WEATHER

The atmosphere is always moving, swirling around over our heads and creating the weather patterns we experience day after day.

Warming Earth
On a warm, sunny day, you can feel the heat from the Sun, which is warming the ground beneath your feet. As the ground warms up, it heats the air above, and this is when the fun starts.

More equal than others
The Sun's energy is not spread evenly over Earth. The Sun's rays hit regions that are close to the poles at oblique (low) angles, and they receive less energy than regions close to the Equator. This helps to make the polar areas cooler than the Equator and this also drives air currents around the planet.

High up the air starts to cool.

Convection current

Cool air

Warm air rises because it is less dense than cold air.

Cold air sinks back down to the ground.

Heat from the ground warms the air.

Warm air

This circular movement is called a **convection current** and we feel this air movement as wind.

Pole

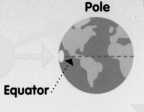

Equator

Equator

And then there's water...
Our planet contains a lot of water and this has an effect on weather patterns. The huge seas absorb a lot of energy from the Sun and can heat up and cool down more quickly than land. This can make coastal areas cooler in summer and warmer in winter than land areas. Water vapour in the air condenses to form clouds and, if the vapour droplets get too big, this falls as rain, snow or hail.

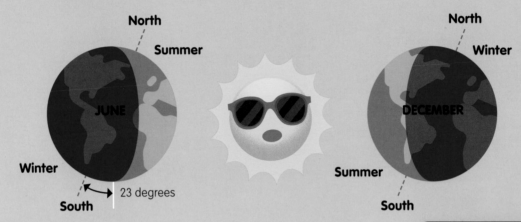

North
Summer
JUNE
Winter
23 degrees
South

North
Winter
DECEMBER
Summer
South

Seasons
Earth does not spin upright in relation to the Sun. instead, Earth is tilted by about 23 degrees, and this tilt creates the different seasons. In June, the Northern Hemisphere is tilted towards the Sun, creating summer, while the Southern Hemisphere is tilted away, creating winter.

In December, the region around the North Pole has 24 hours of darkness, while the region around the South Pole has 24 hours of sunlight.

Coriolis effect
As winds blow across the surface of Earth, the planet's spin drags them to create spiralling movements of air. This is known as the Coriolis effect. It causes tropical storms to rotate anticlockwise in the Northern Hemisphere and clockwise in the Southern Hemisphere.

North
South

Pole

THE WATER CYCLE

Whether it's in the sea, flowing down a river or floating in the sky, water is found all over the planet and it moves in a continual cycle through all its forms; solid ice, liquid water and gassy vapour.

1. Heat from the Sun warms water in oceans, rivers and lakes, evaporating the water and turning it into water vapour.

3. As the air cools, the water vapour condenses, forming clouds.

2. Warm air containing water vapour rises.

8. Some water is absorbed by plants and then released as water vapour.

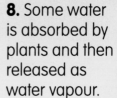

9. Water in streams and rivers flows into lakes and seas.

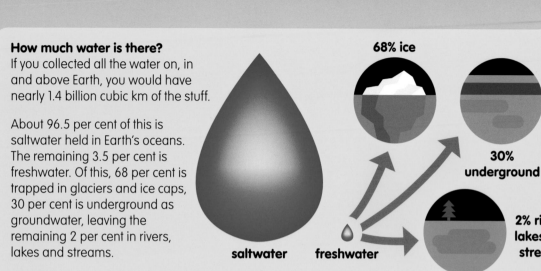

How much water is there?
If you collected all the water on, in and above Earth, you would have nearly 1.4 billion cubic km of the stuff.

About 96.5 per cent of this is saltwater held in Earth's oceans. The remaining 3.5 per cent is freshwater. Of this, 68 per cent is trapped in glaciers and ice caps, 30 per cent is underground as groundwater, leaving the remaining 2 per cent in rivers, lakes and streams.

saltwater   freshwater

68% ice

30% underground

2% rivers, lakes and streams

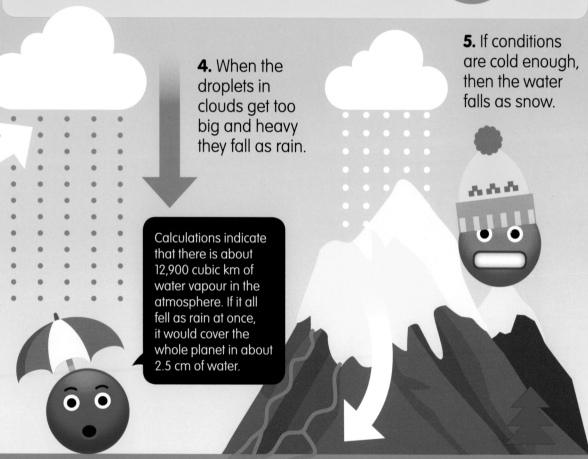

4. When the droplets in clouds get too big and heavy they fall as rain.

5. If conditions are cold enough, then the water falls as snow.

Calculations indicate that there is about 12,900 cubic km of water vapour in the atmosphere. If it all fell as rain at once, it would cover the whole planet in about 2.5 cm of water.

6. Water on the ground flows as surface run-off, joining together to form streams and rivers.

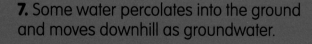

7. Some water percolates into the ground and moves downhill as groundwater.

25

HABITATS

Take the world's range of climates and mix them with its physical features, such as oceans and mountains, and you'll produce a wide range of habitats that play host to Earth's incredible diversity of living organisms.

Rainforests cover about 6 per cent of Earth. Conditions here are warm and wet – perfect for fast-growing trees and an incredible range of wildlife.

Deciduous forests are found in temperate parts of the world, with warm summers and cold winters.

Temperate grasslands cover huge areas of North and South America and Eurasia. Much of these regions has been converted to farmland.

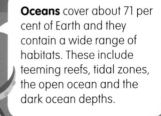

Oceans cover about 71 per cent of Earth and they contain a wide range of habitats. These include teeming reefs, tidal zones, the open ocean and the dark ocean depths.

The high-level habitats of **mountains** are tough places to live, with cold temperatures, harsh weather and lower levels of oxygen in the thin air.

Tropical grasslands have two clear seasons – wet and dry. When the rains fall, huge herds of animals, including zebra and wildebeest, gather to feed on the growing plants.

Taiga, or boreal forest, is the largest land habitat, stretching right around the world, from Alaska, USA, to eastern Siberia, Russia, where temperatures can drop to -50 °C.

Brrrrr! better wrap up warm in the **polar** habitats, where ice and snow cover much of the ground and the only plants are special types of algae.

Deserts receive less than 250 mm of rain a year. They are found in hot tropical regions as well as cooler temperate parts.

Freshwater habitats include rivers, lakes, marshes, bogs and swamps.

CLIMATE CHANGE

Throughout its life, Earth's climate has changed, from cold, frozen periods, called ice ages, where glaciers covered much of the planet, to warmer periods, like the one we're entering now.

Snowball Earth
Some scientists believe that at one time, more than 650 million years ago, the entire Earth was frozen and covered with snow, ice or slush.

1.1 °C is the average increase in the surface temperature of Earth since the late 19th century.

24 cm is the amount sea levels have risen in the last 100 years.

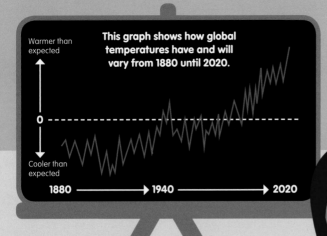

Warmer than expected

This graph shows how global temperatures have and will vary from 1880 until 2020.

0

Cooler than expected

1880   1940   2020

About 97 per cent of climate scientists agree that climate warming over the last 100 years is likely to have been caused by human actions.

Increases in temperatures may have disastrous effects:

The intensity and number of the most powerful **hurricanes** has increased since the early 1980s.

Sea levels are predicted to rise by more than a metre by 2100, flooding low-lying areas and leaving many people homeless.

By the middle of the 21st century, the Arctic may be completely **ice free** during the summer months. This will reduce the living area of many animals that depend on the ice for survival.

Increasing temperatures have led to the melting of the polar ice caps. Between April 2015 and April 2016, the Greenland ice sheet lost about 191 gigatonnes of ice.

Many human activities, such as burning fossil fuels, release carbon dioxide into the atmosphere. Much of this carbon dioxide is absorbed by the planet's oceans, increasing their acidic levels. Since the beginning of the Industrial Revolution in the 18th century, the acidity of Earth's oceans has increased by 30 per cent.

GLOSSARY

ACIDIC
Something with acidic properties, often sour or sharp to taste, with a pH of less than 7.

ASTRONOMER
Someone who studies space and space objects, such as planets, stars and galaxies.

ATMOSPHERE
The layer of mixed gases that surrounds a planet, such as Earth.

AURORAE
Sheets of glowing lights that form high in the atmosphere.

CALDERA
The large crater inside a volcano, often formed when the mouth of a volcano collapses inwards after a big eruption.

CLIMATE
The normal weather conditions for a particular area, which have been consistent over a long period of time.

CONDENSE
The process of changing from a gas or vapour into a liquid.

CONTINENT
One of Earth's seven main landmasses. These are Europe, Asia, Africa, North America, South America, Australia and Antarctica.

DISSOLVE
When a solid substance is incorporated into a liquid, forming a solution.

ELEMENT
A substance that is made up of only one type of atom.

EQUATOR
An imaginary line drawn around the Earth that divides the planet up into northern and southern hemispheres.

EROSION
The natural process of being gradually broken down, caused by moving water and weather. Rivers, wind and rain are common causes of erosion.

FLOODPLAIN
An area that is prone to flooding, often where low-lying ground sits next to a river. Floodplains are usually very fertile and good for growing crops.

FOSSIL FUEL
Natural fuels, such as coal or gas, which have formed in the Earth's crust over very long periods of time.

GLACIER
A slow-moving body of ice that travels down valleys and slopes. Glaciers are often found in high mountain regions and in Earth's coldest climates.

GOLDILOCKS ZONE
The zone around a star (such as our Sun) where life can exist because of the presence of liquid water.

GRAVITY
The force that pulls all objects with mass towards each other.

HABITAT
The natural home of a plant or animal that provides the food and environment it needs to survive.

MAGMA
Extremely hot molten rock that exists below the Earth's surface and sometimes breaks through Earth's crust as a volcanic eruption.

MAGNETIC FIELD
The area of force around a magnet that attracts or repels other magnetic materials.

METEORITE
Solid debris that falls to Earth's surface from outer space.

METEOROID
A small body of rock or metal that travels through the Solar System, but hasn't entered Earth's atmosphere.

OZONE LAYER
A layer of Earth's atmosphere, containing a high amount of ozone (a colourless gas), which absorbs ultraviolet radiation from the Sun.

PERCOLATE
When a liquid or gas filters very slowly through a porous substance.

RADIATION
The transmission of energy in the form of waves or particles. A material can become radioactive if it has an unstable atomic nucleus.

RICHTER SCALE
A scale used to measure the strength or magnitude of earthquakes.

RIVER MOUTH
Where a river reaches another body of water, such as a lake, or the sea.

SEDIMENT
Natural materials, such as sand, which are carried along by water and deposited on a riverbed, or on land.

SEISMIC SHOCKWAVES
The shockwaves produced by earthquakes, which can be detected using seismometers.

TECTONIC PLATES
The large pieces of Earth's crust that are constantly moving. This causes continental drift.

ULTRAVIOLET RADIATION
Invisible electromagnetic radiation that is found naturally in sunlight. Skin responds to ultraviolet radiation by turning darker, which helps protect deeper tissues from damage.

INDEX

Africa 11
Andes 14
Antarctica 11
Arctic 29
Asia 11
Atlantic Ocean 11
atmosphere 20–21, 25
aurorae 7
Australia 11, 15

caldera 13
Chile 12
climate 28–29
clouds 24, 25
continental drift 10–11
continents 10–11
Coriolis effect 23
crust 8, 10–11

deposition 18
deserts 27

earthquakes 9, 12
erosion 18
Europe 11
Everest, Mount 15
exosphere 20

fossil fuels 29
freshwater 25, 27

glaciers 19, 25, 28

habitats 26–27
Himalayas 15
hurricanes 29

ice 24–25, 27, 29
igneous rock 16–17

lava 12–13
life 5

magnetic field 7, 9
mantle 9, 10
Mauna Kea 15
mesosphere 21
metamorphic rock 16–17
meteorites 4, 17
meteors 21
Moon 5
mountains 14–15, 26, 27

North America 11, 27

oceans 4, 25, 26, 29
oxygen 20, 27

Pacific Ocean 12
plate boundaries 12
poles 22, 23, 27

rain 25
rainforests 26
Ring of Fire 12

rivers 18
rock cycle 16–17

seasons 23
sedimentary rock 16–17
snow 25, 27
solar power 7
Solar System 6–7
South America 11, 26
stratosphere 21
Sun 4, 6, 7, 22, 23, 24
supervolcanoes 13

taiga 27
tectonic plates 10, 12, 14
temperate grasslands 26
thermosphere 20
tropical grasslands 27
troposphere 21

valleys 14–15, 19
volcanic mountains 14
volcanoes 12–13, 14

water 23, 24–25
water vapour 24–25
weather 21, 22–23, 28–29
weathering 18
wind 22–23

Yellowstone 13